HORSES & PONIES

ROBERT OWEN

KINGFISHER

For
D F A
and
Oliver

Other books by Robert Owen
My Learn to Ride Book
Successful Riding and Jumping
The Country Life Book of the Horse
Riding and Jumping
Learning to Ride
Horse and Pony Dictionary
The Young Rider (with John Bullock)

Artists
Julie Chandler
T Crosby-Smith
Gary Rees
Peter Swann-Brown
Tudor Art
Janos Maffrey

Kingfisher Books
New Penderel House
283–288 High Holborn
London WC1V 7HZ

First published in paperback by Kingfisher 1997
10 9 8 7 6 5 4 3 2
First published in hardback by Kingfisher 1978
Reprinted 1991
© Grisewood & Dempsey Limited 1978, 1991
© Text Robert Owen 1978, 1991

A CIP record for this book is available from the British Library

ISBN 0 7534 0204 1

Phototypeset by Wyvern 21 Limited
Printed in Hong Kong by
South China Printing Company (1988) Limited

Above: *Icelandic ponies*

Below:*One of the many important tasks undertaken by any rider is to clean items of saddlery and tack*

Contents

Acknowledgements

The publishers wish to thank the following for supplying photographs for this book:

Cover: Kit Houghton
Endpapers: ZEFA
Page 4 ZEFA; 7 ZEFA (*top*); 9 ZEFA; 10 Kit Houghton (*top*), National Gallery, London (*bottom*); 11 ZEFA; 12 Sally Anne Thompson / Animal Photography (*top*), Mansell Collection (*centre*); 13 ZEFA; 14 Sally Anne Thompson / Animal Photography; 15 Sally Anne Thompson / Animal Photography, ZEFA (*bottom left*); 16 ZEFA, Sonia Halliday (*bottom left*); 18 Kit Houghton; 19 Kit Houghton (*right*); 20 Kit Houghton (*top*); 25 Kit Houghton; 28 Sally Anne Thompson / Animal Photography (*top*), ZEFA (*centre*), E.D. Lacey (*bottom*); 31 Sally Anne Thompson / Animal Photography; 32 Kit Houghton; 36 Kit Houghton (*top*), Sally Anne Thompson / Animal Photography (*centre*); 38 Kit Houghton (*bottom*): 39 Kit Houghton; 40 Kit Houghton (*bottom*); 41 Kit Houghton; 43 ZEFA (*left*), Kit Houghton (*right*); 44 Kit Houghton; 45 E.D. Lacey (*top*), ZEFA (*centre*), SATOUR (*bottom*); 46 Kit Houghton; 47 E.D. Lacey (*top left*), Kit Houghton (*top and bottom left*), ZEFA (*bottom right*); 48 Syndication International (*top*), Kit Houghton (*bottom*); 49 Kit Houghton (*top*); 50 Kit Houghton; 51 E.D. Lacey (*top*), Kit Houghton (*bottom*); 52 ZEFA; 53 ZEFA (*top*), E.D. Lacey (*middle and bottom*); 54 ZEFA (*top and middle*), Spectrum Colour Library (*bottom left*), 55 ZEFA (*top and bottom left*), The Post Office (*bottom right*); ZEFA (*top*), Syndication International (*bottom left*), Government of Alberta (*bottom right*); 57 Syndication International (*top*), ZEFA (*bottom*); 58 Syndication International (*bottom*); 59 Syndication International (*top*);

All other photographs by Robert Owen.

Picture Research: Elaine Willis

Introduction

In recent years riding, and everything involved with the care and keeping of horses and ponies, has become a very popular activity. Throughout the world millions of people are active in one part or another of the equestrian scene, and a great percentage of these are younger people.

For some, riding is the perfect competitive sport. There is always an element of the unknown – horses and ponies are not finely tuned machines. The horse demands a personal commitment and daily care and attention, and the learning process never stops.

Through television, viewers can now see top riders and their horses in a great variety of competition. Many also enjoy the atmosphere of the show scene and watch horse shows and events from the ring side.

Horses and Ponies is not a manual or handbook; it is a guide to the world of horses and ponies, giving an outline to help both those who already ride or who are learning to ride, and the many others who help at riding establishments or stable yards.

The book falls into four parts, beginning with a brief note about the horse and the difficult subject of conformation. After discussing a few of the more than two hundred breeds, the book looks at the problems and pleasures of horse or pony ownership.

The second part explains the tasks which must be accepted by all who take on the responsibility of caring for animals. It is their welfare and well-being which must be considered at all times.

Horses and Ponies then looks at what is entailed in beginning to ride. This part includes an introduction to saddlery and tack, bits and bridles, and the items of equipment and clothing needed by stable-kept and grass-kept horses and ponies.

The final part covers competitive sports – showing, showjumping, dressage, eventing and carriage driving – and ends with a look at horses at work and horses in sport.

In these pages are some carefully selected all-colour photographs and drawings, showing why those involved with horses and ponies have so much to think about and enjoy every hour of every day.

About the horse

What is conformation?

The more a rider learns about horses and ponies, the more frequently he or she hears the word 'conformation'. It is heard during riding lessons, in the stable yard, inside and outside showing or jumping arenas, and in conversation with other riders or owners. Conformation is basically another word for structure and shape. It is used in the horse world to describe the way in which animals are 'put together'. In other words, it means the appearance of the horse or pony, with all its good and bad points.

Studying conformation is a way of making a judgement between one horse and another. It is a complicated subject and it takes many years to understand fully everything that is included.

Left: *This photograph is worth close study. The horse has many excellent features and good conformation*

Below left: *From a painting by the equestrian artist George Stubbs (1724–1806), in the National Gallery, London*

Right: *All who enjoy being with horses and ponies should know the* points of the horse, *many of which are illustrated. These are frequently mentioned in a riding school or stable yard*

When you begin to look for your own horse or pony, you should consider just what experience you have, both as a rider and as someone who will be looking after a horse and pony. Have a clear picture in your mind of your 'ideal' animal – but first make sure that you have all the facilities required. *Never* take on the responsibility of ownership until you are certain you can cope with all it involves

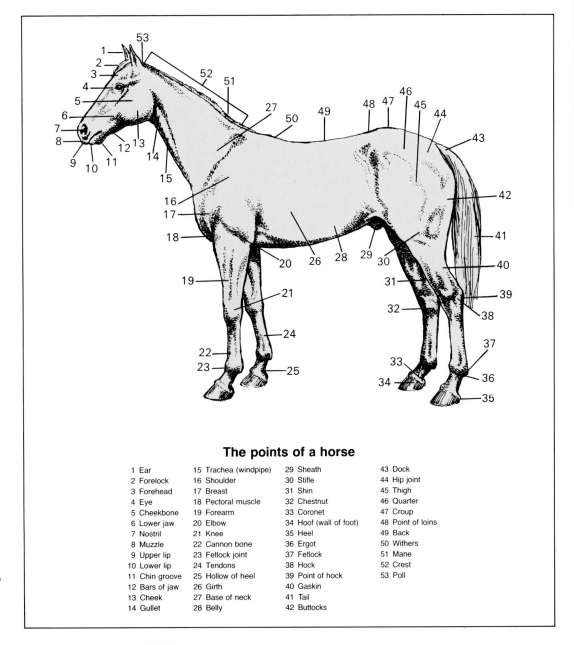

The points of a horse

1 Ear	15 Trachea (windpipe)	29 Sheath	43 Dock
2 Forelock	16 Shoulder	30 Stifle	44 Hip joint
3 Forehead	17 Breast	31 Shin	45 Thigh
4 Eye	18 Pectoral muscle	32 Chestnut	46 Quarter
5 Cheekbone	19 Forearm	33 Coronet	47 Croup
6 Lower jaw	20 Elbow	34 Hoof (wall of foot)	48 Point of loins
7 Nostril	21 Knee	35 Heel	49 Back
8 Muzzle	22 Cannon bone	36 Ergot	50 Withers
9 Upper lip	23 Fetlock joint	37 Fetlock	51 Mane
10 Lower lip	24 Tendons	38 Hock	52 Crest
11 Chin groove	25 Hollow of heel	39 Point of hock	53 Poll
12 Bars of jaw	26 Girth	40 Gaskin	
13 Cheek	27 Base of neck	41 Tail	
14 Gullet	28 Belly	42 Buttocks	

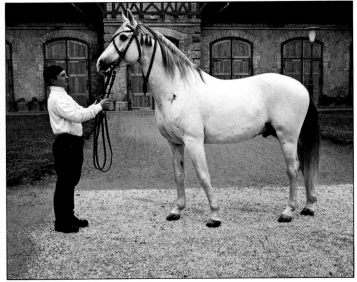

What should be looked for?

When first looking at a horse or pony, you must consider its overall appearance and general characteristics (its *conformation*). You should then look more closely at a number of specific points – the head and the way it is set; the eyes; the neck; shoulders; withers; quarters; legs and feet. You must also look at how the horse moves. What is its 'action'? Is the stride pattern good? How are the transitions made from one pace to another?

With experience, riders acquire the ability to see immediately what is good or bad in a horse or pony's conformation. Making this judgement is not easy, but it is a skill young riders will gain with time and knowledge.

Breeds

Breeds and breeding can seem a difficult and technical subject which is best left to experts. However, anyone interested in horses and ponies should have some knowledge of breeds.

There are more than 200 recognized breeds throughout the world. Many have their own Breed Societies, which keep registers or stud books listing certain horses or ponies. These animals have been carefully and selectively bred, and show clearly defined characteristics of the breed, including conformation, height, colour and action. As well as the established breeds, there are a number of horses known as 'types'. Hunters, cobs, hacks, riding and polo ponies are all types of horse or pony.

From Eohippus to the Thoroughbred

The earliest ancestor of the horse was the Eohippus, an animal about the size of a fox with four toes. Several millions of years later, the horse we recognize today, called Equus, first appeared in North America.

The **Arab**, about which much is known, is perhaps the oldest and purest of the *breeds* we know today. Carvings of this horse dating from about 1500BC have been found in Egypt and the Middle East. More recently, the **Andalusian** breed from Spain played a large part in the development of breeds and breeding.

During the 18th century the famous English **Thoroughbred** was established by crossing selected home-bred mares with three Arab stallions – the Darley Arabian, the Godolphin Arabian and the Byerley Turk. Today the Thoroughbred has been crossed with many other breeds.

From left to right: *A pony; a type of horse suitable for most equestrian activities; two heavier horses*

Left, top: *A beautifully proportioned Arab showing excellent conformation*

Left, centre: *An engraving from 1823 of the Darley Arabian, an Arab stallion brought to England by Thomas Darley in 1704. The Darley Arabian was, with two other imported Arabians (the Byerley Turk and the Godolphin Arabian) one of the founder sires of the English Thoroughbred. It was a pure-bred Arab of the Managhi line*

Above: *Mares grazing with a foal*

Right: *The standards of the Palomino breed have been established by the Palomino Horse Association. Palominos stand between 14 and 16hh. The body colour is golden, with a full white mane and tail*

Below: *The forebears of the Icelandic pony probably came to Iceland with early Norwegian settlers.*

1 There are four sections of **Welsh pony**, ranging from the smallest, Section A, which stands up to 12hh to the Welsh Cob (standing up to 15.3hh)

2 The **Exmoor** is the oldest of the nine British native breeds of pony. It stands up to 12.2hh and can carry very heavy weights. It is used as a foundation stock for breeding bigger horses

3 The **American Standardbred** is a muscular horse, not quite so refined as the Thoroughbred. It has a free and straight action and is widely used in trotting races. The Standardbred is found in all main colours. It is descended from a foal of the Darley Arabian.

4 The hunter **type** is able to carry riders of all weights over all types of country. Their temperament and ability make them ideal showing animals. They are usually half-bred, though most have some percentage of Thoroughbred blood

5 The smallest of all pony breeds comes from the Shetland Islands north of Scotland. **Shetland ponies** are measured in inches rather than hands. To be registered in the Breed Register, a Shetland pony must not be taller than 42in

(107cm)

6 The **Connemara** has become well-loved as a family pony. They are sturdy, reliable and highly intelligent

7 The **Morgan**, one of the most popular and versatile breeds from the United States, was named after Justin Morgan who lived at the beginning of the 19th century. They stand between 14.2 and 15.2hh and are usually black, brown, bay or chestnut

8 The **Hanoverian** developed from Oriental and Andulusian stallions crossed with local mares. Since the mid-1730s many English Thoroughbreds have been used in the breeding. Hanoverians are highly talented and are used for showjumping, eventing and dressage

9 The **Lipizanner**, primarily a high school horse, has been made famous throughout the world by the renowned Spanish Riding School in Vienna. They are mostly grey and come from Lipizza, a village in the north-west of Yugoslavia

10 The **Breton**, a light draught horse from France, combines alertness with immense stamina

5

6

7

8

9

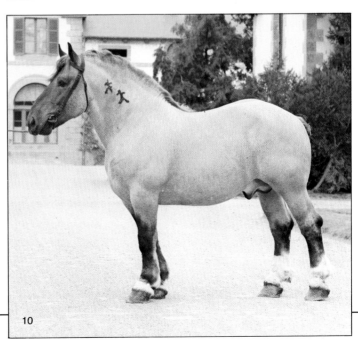

10

Colours

The principal colours of horses and ponies are black, brown, bay, chestnut and grey. There is no 'white' horse – an animal with a very light coat is described as light grey. Other colours and mixtures of colours include dun, roan, piebald and skewbald. Colour combinations outside these are known as 'odd-coloured'.

During the first year of a horse's life, the body colour (*pigmentation*) begins to change, and its so-called 'true' colour will not emerge until late in its second year. It is interesting that the coat of many black foals will grow out to become grey. If doubt arises over a horse's true colour (sometimes required for a Breed Society or for use on a horse passport), reference is made to the colour of the hairs in the muzzle, tips of the ears, the mane and tail.

Above: *A bay horse has a brown body with black mane and tail. Some black appears on the limbs*

Below: *In a dun-coloured horse the body colour will vary from cream to a shade of yellow. Most duns have a black line (the* dorsal) *running along the spine and a black mane and tail*

Above: *A chestnut has a reddish colour of coat with a similar colour of mane and tail. There are three variations of chestnut – light, dark and liver.*
A black horse has a black mane and tail. No other colour is accepted, apart from some white markings

Below: *In Britain a piebald horse or pony has a coat showing irregular patches and shapes of white and black. A skewbald has large and irregular white patches, on any colour other than black.*
Other colour combinations of a horse or pony are known as 'odd-coloured'

Above: *A brown horse has a dark brown coat which may at times look black. They invariably have black points*

Below: *Cream horses have a light coloured coat with unpigmented skin. The eyes of a cream horse are pink or blue. A grey's coat has a mixture of black and grey-white hairs*

Markings

Although horses and ponies are described by the colour of their coats, their markings are also identifying features. Markings appear principally on the body, head and legs. Where no markings are to be seen, the horse is known as 'whole-coloured'.

At times markings can easily be confused with colours. For example, a 'spotted' horse, such as an **Appaloosa**, has spots mainly across its quarters, although they also occur all over the body and limbs. Some people wrongly call all spotted horses Appaloosas; it is, however, a recognized breed, as is the **Knabstrup** from Denmark.

A 'flecked' horse or pony is marked with small collections of white-coloured hairs appearing irregularly over the body. The zebra-marked horse is very much as its name suggests, the marks showing on the shoulders, back, quarters and legs.

Another colour/marking combination is found on the **Pinto**, a breed from the United States. The word Pinto comes from a Spanish word, *pintado*, meaning painted – a true description of a most beautiful breed.

Any horse or pony with a 'dorsal' stripe will show a continuous line running along the spine from mane to tail.

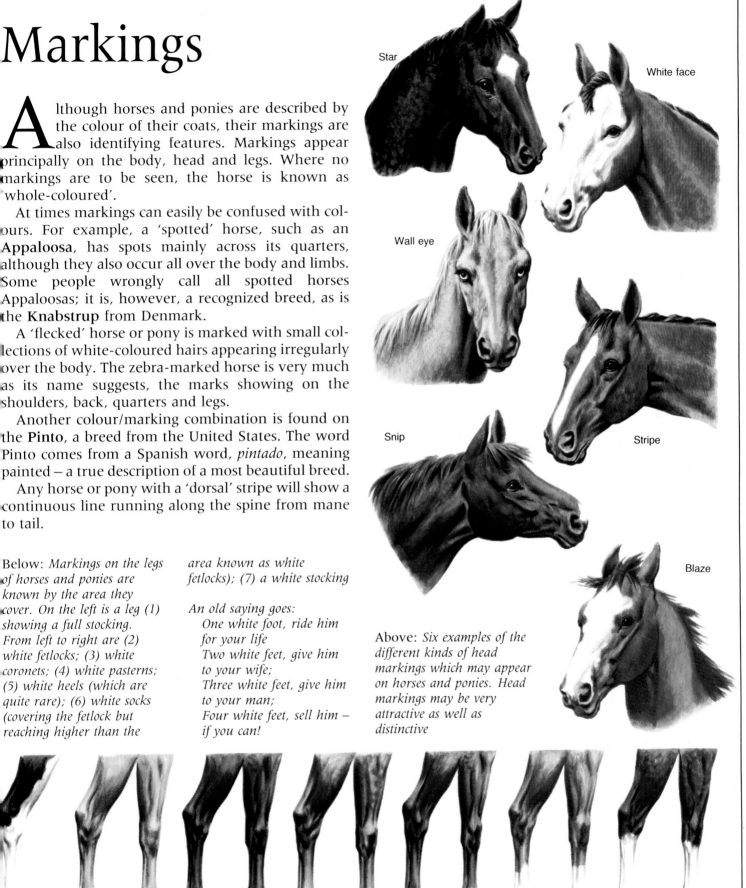

Below: *Markings on the legs of horses and ponies are known by the area they cover. On the left is a leg (1) showing a full stocking. From left to right are (2) white fetlocks; (3) white coronets; (4) white pasterns; (5) white heels (which are quite rare); (6) white socks (covering the fetlock but reaching higher than the* area known as white fetlocks); (7) a white stocking

An old saying goes:
> One white foot, ride him for your life
> Two white feet, give him to your wife;
> Three white feet, give him to your man;
> Four white feet, sell him – if you can!

Above: *Six examples of the different kinds of head markings which may appear on horses and ponies. Head markings may be very attractive as well as distinctive*

The veterinary surgeon

Veterinary medicine concerns itself with the study, prevention and treatment of animal diseases. The training to become a veterinary surgeon takes many years. All those involved with horses will have occasion to call for the vet, but anyone looking after horses and ponies should also know something about treating simple ailments.

Perhaps the most important call to the vet will be when you ask him or her to examine a horse or pony before you agree to buy. This examination will include the condition of the lungs and respiration; the heart and pulse rate; the condition of the eyes (very important signals to a vet); a check of the teeth, and confirmation that the horse or pony's action is 'level'. The vet will also check for signs of weakness or injury. A veterinary certificate will show the results.

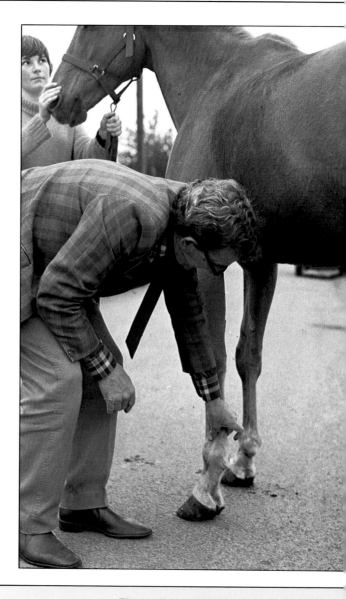

Below: *The veterinary surgeon is seen using a stethoscope, much as it would be used on humans by a doctor. The stethoscope is an instrument which brings sounds in the chest to the examiner's ear*

Right: *A veterinary surgeon examines the leg of a horse to feel for signs of weakness. He will also check for signs of injury. No vet will pass a horse if there is any sign that the legs are not sound*

The medicine cabinet

Many of the common ailments affecting horses and ponies can be treated by 'first aid' in the stable. But **never** hesitate to call the vet if any doubt exists.
All stables should keep a medicine cabinet, and a smaller medicine box should be carried in a horse box or trailer.
A list of possible items to be kept in the cabinet include:

A pair of blunt-ended surgical scissors. Some calico bandages. A roll or two of cotton wool. Some packets of lint. A roll or two of gamgee tissue.

Some small packets of oiled silk. Surgical tape. Safety pins. One or two colic drinks which can be supplied by your vet. A bottle of embrocation. Some Witch

Hazel and a tin of kaolin. A jar of cough electuary. A tin of antibiotic dusting powder. A jar or tin of Epsom salts. A bottle of glycerine.

Make a regular habit of checking the contents of both the medicine cabinet and travelling box, replacing items which have been used. Do not keep medicines for too long: see that everything is clean and fresh

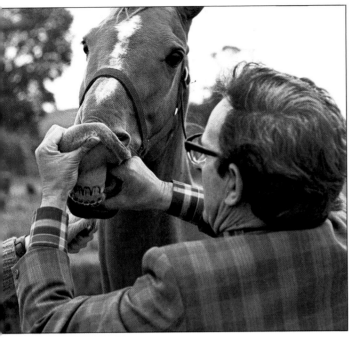

Left: *A horse's mouth is not difficult to open, despite what some people think, but great care must be taken when examining teeth*

Below: *The action of a horse or pony can be checked by having the animal walked away and returned in a straight line*

up to six months

two years

three years

five years

seven years

nine years

fifteen years

twenty-five years

Above: *The age of a horse is determined by the shape and marks found on the teeth. Milk teeth appear some 10 days after birth. The teeth then develop with marked characteristics at certain ages. When the animal reaches the age of 15 years it becomes difficult to determine the exact age*

A vet may suggest a further, more detailed examination, possibly obtaining a number of X-rays, before advising whether or not the animal is suitable for the buyer's purpose.

Questions the vet may ask

Veterinary surgeons like to feel a particular horse or pony is ideally suited, and they may ask certain questions before carrying out an initial examination. The vet may ask what experience the buyer has in looking after a horse or pony. For what riding activity is the animal to be used? Will it be kept at livery? Will it be kept at grass or stable-kept? What grazing is available, and what is the condition of the land? How much is known about feeding practice?

When you need to call a vet, make sure you can give a clear indication of where you think the trouble is, and for how long there have been signs that all is not well. All kinds of illnesses, injuries and signs of stress arise during the lifetime of every horse. Some ailments can be treated without calling the vet, but where there is **any doubt**, never hesitate to obtain the best advice and treatment possible.

Buying a horse or pony

There is no easy or straightforward path when buying a horse or pony. It is never simple, but it can be very exciting and rewarding – especially when buying for the first time.

Horses and ponies change owners in several ways. In some countries horses are seldom advertised, but this method is most commonly used in Britain, Australia, New Zealand and the United States. Horse 'sales' are usually held on market days or at horse fairs, or you can go to a reputable dealer.

For many people, it is best to look for a horse or pony whose temperament and ability you already know. Riders and owners frequently have to change – a young rider may have outgrown a pony, or a horse owner may decide to give up or to move into another form of equestrian activity. An alternative method of buying is to place your own advertisement in 'wanted' columns. This gives you the chance to describe exactly what you are seeking; breed, height, colour, age and experience. Ask for details and a photograph, remembering that nothing can be final until you have seen the animal and obtained your vet's certificate.

Below: *A careful examination of a horse or pony is most important in considering whether to buy. Before calling the vet to carry out this examination, you should also have the horse ridden-out by the seller to show paces and general ability. The prospective buyer should also ride to make sure the animal is suitable. Check that the horse or pony has been trained to go out on roads and highways, and will go quietly into a box or trailer*

Above: *One method of buying, though not the best for the inexperienced, is at a horse market or horse sale. Horses and ponies are also sold at horse 'fairs'*

The standard measurement of height for a horse or pony is the **hand**. One hand (sometimes written *hh*) is equal to 4in (10cm). It is becoming the normal practice in Europe, however, to give heights in *metric* measure. The British Show Jumping Association follows the way set by the FEI (*Fédération Equestre Internationale*), one of whose Rules states that 'an animal which exceeds 148cm cannot be accepted for registration as a pony.'

For an accurate measurement, the horse or pony is measured without shoes, standing on level ground. The height is the distance from ground level to the highest point of the horse's withers. Where an animal with shoes is measured, an allowance of $\frac{1}{2}$in (12mm) is taken off the height.

Among the signs of a healthy pony are:

He will feed up well
He will be alert and interested in all that goes on around him
He will stand squarely
He will be seen to enjoy his work and periods of rest

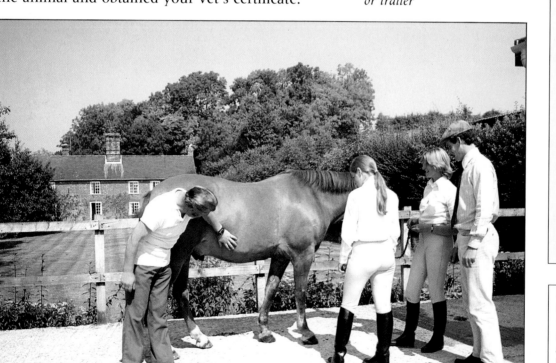

Care of the horse

Looking after the welfare of a horse or pony means far more than simply seeing it is fed and watered. Your daily routine should begin with an early morning inspection to check for any signs of lameness or illness. Only then can the work of stable management begin.

In the paddock

The state of the fencing or hedging should be checked at regular intervals to see that nothing is broken and that no gaps have appeared. Any plants which can be dangerous to horses and ponies (see page 22) should be dug up and destroyed. The paddock and shelter must be kept clean for reasons of hygiene, and all droppings removed daily to the muck heap. The water trough will also require checking to ensure there is always plenty of fresh, clean water, not just in the summer months but throughout the year.

Feeding practice

Grass-kept horses and ponies who are undertaking even gentle work will need hay in addition to their grazing. Protein can be given in the form of pony nuts, and other feeds may include corn, chaff, bran, linseed and extra vitamins. In autumn and winter a horse will require larger quantities of hay. In the spring, when grazing is fresh and lush, care must be taken to see that no animal is over-grazing.

The feeding routine for a stable-kept horse depends largely on the work it does. Some general rules of good feeding are: feed *little* and *often*; if possible, allow some grazing every day; make sure that there is sufficient bulk feed, such as hay; feed at the same time each day; never make sudden changes to the feed being given; never work immediately after feeding; feed according to work being done, and water before feeding.

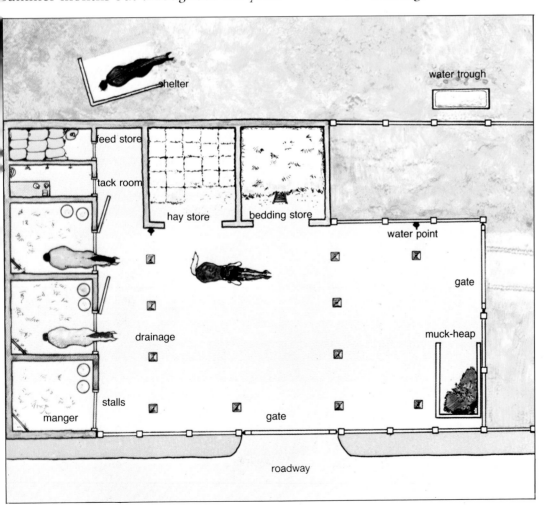

Left: *It is almost impossible to illustrate a 'perfect' stable area. Owners have their own ideas as to how a stable yard should be laid out, and much depends on the site, the position of a roadway, the access to the paddocks, and the number of horses being stabled.*
Note here the position of the feed store and hay and bedding stores in relation to the muck-heap. Keep the siting of a muck-heap away from the stables, but make sure it can be emptied without difficulty.
An ideal yard must have good drainage. The plan suggests a line of drains placed near the roadside boundary. This is necessary for ensuring the yard can be kept clean, and is essential in some areas to comply with local bye-laws.
The yard, looseboxes and stores must always be kept neat and tidy. Cleanliness and hygiene are essential in the stable yard

Above: *Barbed wire, used as a form of fencing, is something to be avoided. All fencing and hedging to paddocks must be regularly checked, and any broken sections repaired. The ideal type of fencing is post-and-rail, built high enough to keep horses and ponies enclosed*

Right: *Check daily that the ball-cock allows a flow of fresh water into the trough*

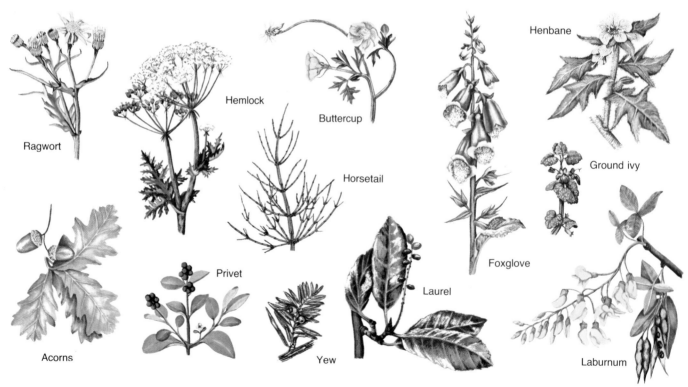

Ragwort

Hemlock

Buttercup

Horsetail

Henbane

Ground ivy

Foxglove

Acorns

Privet

Yew

Laurel

Laburnum

Above: *Some plants, weeds, and the leaves and fruits of trees and shrubs can be dangerous to horses and ponies if eaten in excess.*

Keep a constant watch on what is growing in or near the fields and paddocks. Hedgerows surrounding a field might contain all sorts of dangerous growth. One of the most common weeds, ragwort, is particularly dangerous, especially when pulled up and left to die on the ground. All plants and weeds which are dangerous must be dug up and destroyed, not left to decompose on the muck heap

Right: Soiled straw should be removed with a fork. The straw to be removed is separated from the dry bedding and taken to the muck-heap. The process of 'mucking-out' must be carried out every morning. As long as the horse is tied up, and has his morning hay net, he will stand quietly while the work is being done

Rugs

Those who care for horses and ponies must know something about the use of items of protective clothing. Rugs are used at all times for animals whether they are stable-kept, kept at grass or travelling. They are needed during all seasons of the year, and during daytime and through the nights.

The following are among the many types available:

New Zealand: a waterproof canvas rug with a blanket lining.

Day rug: usually made from wool. The picture on page 31 shows a horse wearing a day rug prior to travelling.

Night rug: used over a blanket and made from jute or canvas. It is best to use a woollen blanket under a night rug.

Lavenham rug: a quilted, lightweight rug which can be used during all seasons.

Anti-sweat sheet: made from cotton mesh to prevent a sudden chill.

Summer sheet: used mainly to keep away flies.

Right: Part of a clean and tidy-looking tack room. See how neatly the cleaned saddles are kept. In the background are some bridles, also clean and ready for use. All saddlery is expensive and must be treated with care. There should be a place in a tack room for each item of equipment, from bandages, leathers, reins, stirrups and girths to larger items such as saddles, bridles and rugs

23

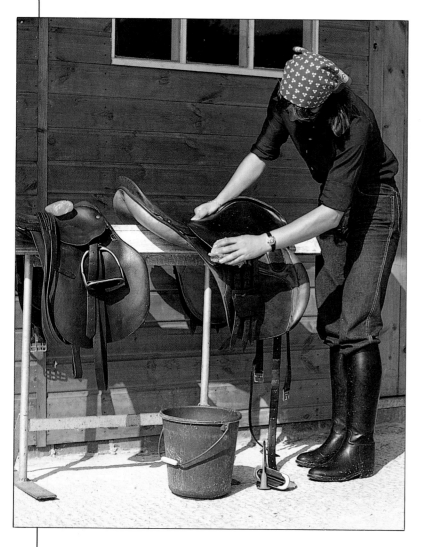

Cleaning saddlery

All items of saddlery, and other necessary equipment, are expensive to buy or to replace, so it is important to keep everything in good order. Tack should be cleaned after every ride or exercise period to preserve the leather and keep equipment ready for use.

Before cleaning, separate all parts of a saddle or bridle. Then remove the dirt and grease with a soft sponge, dampened in cold or slightly warm water. Allow the leather to dry off naturally before applying saddle soap with another sponge. From time to time use neatsfoot oil or a leather preservative. **Never** use hot water or a detergent to clean leather, and never try to speed up the drying process by placing wet leather near a fire or radiator. This will dry everything too quickly, and take away the natural oils. Clean metal items with slightly warm water, and rub with a metal polish or impregnated cloth.

During the cleaning process, take a good look at the condition of the stitching. Make sure there are no signs of wear – broken or worn stitching can easily be the cause of an accident. It is also advisable to check bits for signs of roughness which might damage the horse's mouth.

Grooming

Grooming is the *daily* attention given to the coat, skin, mane, tail and feet of all stable-kept horses and

Above: *A bucket of clean water, a bar of saddle soap and two sponges are required to clean saddles properly.*

This photograph shows the use made of a saddle stand Below: *Clean the body brush by using a curry comb*

Below: *One of the two sponges used in grooming should be kept for cleaning the eyes and muzzle*

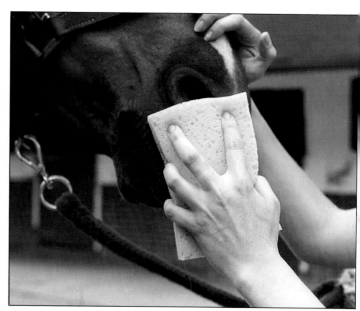

ponies. Proper grooming aims to promote health, prevent disease, maintain condition, improve appearance, and ensure cleanliness.

When grooming a stable-kept horse or pony, begin by picking out the feet with a *hoof pick*, working downwards from the heel towards the toe. Remove all dirt and look closely to see that all is well. Check that the shoes are not badly worn, and feel for risen clenches – both of these may cause the horse injury. When grooming the body, begin by using the *dandy brush*, especially around the saddle area, head, points of the hocks, fetlocks and pasterns. Then take the *body brush* in one hand and a *curry comb* in the other. Work over the entire body, including the mane, with short circular strokes rather than with an up and down motion. After every five or six strokes, draw the brush across the comb to dislodge the accumulated dirt. When using the body brush, take particular care as you groom the more tender parts of the body. Finally, use the *wisp* as a form of massage and body toning. Sponging of the eyes and muzzle is one part of grooming enjoyed by most horses and ponies. A second sponge is used to clean the whole of the dock area.

When grooming animals kept at grass, it is essential that natural greases are not removed during the winter months. A different method of grooming is therefore adopted. Use the dandy brush, or sometimes a rubber curry comb, to remove caked mud from the legs and lower part of the body. Do not go over the body with a body brush. Each day, as with the stable-kept horse, the feet must be picked out and a general inspection made. In all weathers the eyes, muzzle and dock regions should be sponged and kept clean.

Illustrated opposite are items found in a grooming kit. These are:

the *hoof pick*, used for picking out the feet

the *dandy brush*, used for removing caked mud, heavy dirt and dust. It is invaluable for use on the grass-kept horse or pony

the *body brush*, will remove dust, scurf and dandruff from the coat, mane and tail

the *curry comb*, made from metal or rubber, is used for cleaning the body brush. Also used for removing caked mud from animals kept at grass

the *water brush*, when dampened, is used on the mane, tail and feet

the *sponges* (there should be at least two) are used with clean water: one sponge for the eyes and muzzle: the other for the dock area

the *wisp* promotes circulation and helps tone up the muscles

the *stable rubber* adds a final polish after grooming

Water brush   Dandy brush

Body brush

Hoof-pick   Curry comb

Comb

Stable rubber

Cleaning material with sponge and duster

Above: *Some of the items which form part of a grooming kit*

Below: *This horse, without a headcollar, is coming to hand by being offered some pony nuts*

The farrier

The old saying 'no foot, no horse' is as true today as ever. A horse or pony without sound feet is, sadly, a useless and most unhappy animal. When feet have been neglected, it is a slow process to full recovery and normal action. Not even farriers, with all their skill, can be expected to put things right. There is much that they can do, but the responsibility for keeping feet in good condition belongs to the person looking after a horse or pony.

Shoes quickly become worn or lost (*cast*) and the walls of the feet grow. If that growth is not trimmed back, a horse will go lame. Neglected feet upset balance and cause strain to ligaments, joints and tendons.

It is very important to check the feet every day. Most shoes need replacing every five or six weeks.

Below: *The farrier brings the heated shoe to the anvil and shapes it by using either a 'cross pin' or 'cat's head' hammer. Next the nail holes are made with a 'stamp', a tool with a sharpened end the same size as the heads of the nails used to fix the shoe*

Above: *Among the tools shown on the farrier's apron are: the driving hammer; buffer; pritchel; pincers; 'searcher'; toe knife; rasp; pincers and nails*

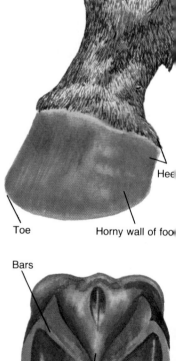

Toe

Heel

Horny wall of foot

Bars

Sole

Frog

Wall

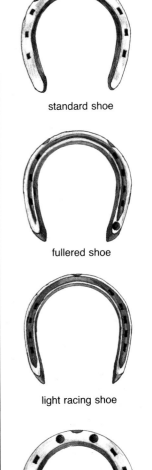

standard shoe

fullered shoe

light racing shoe

shoe for draught horse

1 The farrier first 'knocks up' or cuts off the clenches with a hammer and the end of his buffer. The shoe is then tapped until it can be lifted by the pincers

2 Starting at the heel, the old shoe is levered off by pulling it down towards the toe. This work must not be hurried: great care is taken to avoid damaging the walls of the feet

3 Once the old shoe has been removed, dirt and any growth is cleaned from the foot with the blunt side of the 'searcher' or drawing knife

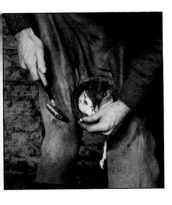

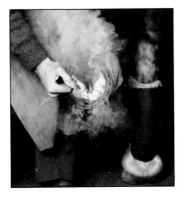

4 Finally the foot is rasped flat and level to ensure equal distribution of weight on all parts of the foot once the shoe is fitted

5 When the new shoe has been made, it will be taken from the fire by means of a 'pritchel' and placed on the foot. The horse feels no discomfort. After the foot is scorched, the clips are cut

6 If the shoe does not fit it will be taken back to the anvil to be adjusted. The shoe is cooled before fitting and the nail holes checked to make certain the shape and fit are accurate

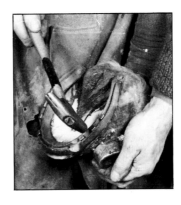

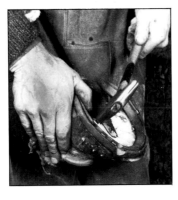

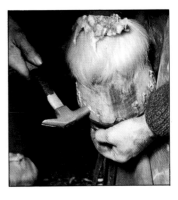

7 The new shoe is nailed on with the driving hammer – starting at the toe. The inside nails are hammered in first, the last one being that on the outside of the heel

8 The protruding nail can be seen in this picture. The farrier will have made seven nail holes in the shoe: four on the outside edge and three on the inside edge

9 The nails are then tightened-up by placing the pincers under the end of each nail (the clenches). These are 'wrung-off' and each nail is then hammered tightly home

10 The 'clenches' are turned over and tapped into the wall of the foot. Finally, the outside of the wall is rasped to get rid of any sharp edges

Saddlery

For most people, saddlery means the basic items used in riding – the saddle, bridle and reins. But the word actually covers *all* the items of equipment which clothe the horse and enable the rider to maintain control.

Two important points about saddlery must be clear – all items (sometimes referred to as **tack**) must be *safe* and must *fit*. This may seem obvious, but horses and ponies are frequently seen with ill-fitting saddlery. No horse can perform well unless the equipment it is wearing fits properly and is comfortable.

Today, there is a confusing range of saddlery available. Saddlery and tack have changed over recent years, with the introduction of plastics and artificial fibres.

Ever since people first domesticated the horse, they have needed to find a way of controlling it. So forms of bridle were adopted, and a type of saddle introduced for comfort. The principles of saddlery have not changed much over the centuries, but saddles and bridles are now designed for specific equestrian activities.

It is essential that all saddlery fits properly, and the saddler is the best person to check this. The checking of tack can only be carried out when the rider is mounted. The points to look for are:

to make certain there is no pressure on the spine of the horse or pony
to check that no weight falls on the horse's loins
to see that the weight of the rider is evenly distributed over the muscles covering the rib cage
to check that the pommel of the saddle is not pressing down on the horse's withers

Below: *Three types of girth. From top to bottom: a leather girth, a girth made from webbing, a nylon cord girth*

Bottom, right: *A racing saddle is light in weight and has a small saddle flap. Jockeys ride with very short leathers*

Below: *A young rider is seen mounted with a show saddle. This has been specially made to show to best advantage the shoulders of the grey pony*

Centre: *Riding with a Western saddle. It will be noticed how long the leathers are, especially when compared to the racing picture below*

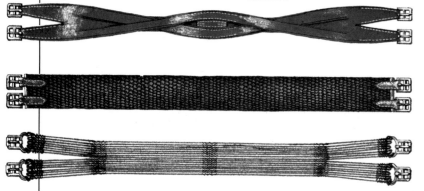

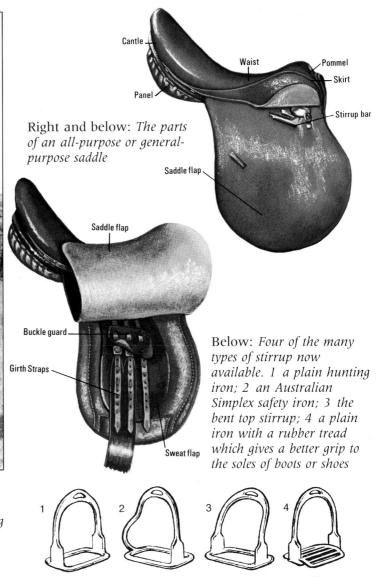

Cantle

Waist

Pommel

Skirt

Panel

Stirrup bar

Right and below: *The parts of an all-purpose or general-purpose saddle*

Saddle flap

Saddle flap

Buckle guard

Girth Straps

Sweat flap

Below: *Four of the many types of stirrup now available. 1 a plain hunting iron; 2 an Australian Simplex safety iron; 3 the bent top stirrup; 4 a plain iron with a rubber tread which gives a better grip to the soles of boots or shoes*

1   2   3   4

Above: *Oakwood Zeltah, a magnificent black horse, sired by an Anglo-Arab from a Russian mare, stands at 16.2 hands (168 cm). The rider is using an all-purpose* or general-purpose saddle, *suitable for various equestrian activities including hunting, hacking, showjumping, eventing or showing*

PUTTING ON A SADDLE

Below: *Remain on the near side, take the girth from under the horse's belly and buckle up. Check that all is well by looking at both sides, then the stirrups can be 'run down'*

Above: *Approach from the near side, carrying the saddle across the right arm. Give the horse or pony a reassuring touch on the shoulder*

Right: *Place the saddle gently on the highest part of the withers. Then slide the saddle back to the correct position. When saddling it is best if the horse or pony is tied-up*

The bridle

The bridle is used to support the bit or bits to which the reins are attached. By correct use of the reins, through the hands, the rider is able to control pace and direction. The hands are also a means of communication between rider and horse. However, there can be no control or communication until the rider's hands, body-weight, and legs (see page 32) are correctly used in *conjunction* with each other.

There are five main groups of bridle – the snaffle, the Weymouth or double bridle, the Pelham, the Gag and the Hackamore. Each kind is made up of several pieces – the headpiece, cheekpieces, browband, noseband and selected bit. The simplest and most widely used is the snaffle with its single rein and either a jointed or straight bit. The Weymouth and Pelham have double reins, the Weymouth combining a bradoon (snaffle) bit with a curb chain. The Pelham, though not the most suitable for younger riders, is popular with many, especially in the showing ring. It combines the action of the snaffle with a curb. The Hackamore or bitless bridle, like the Gag, is only suitable for experienced riders.

Above: *Always put on a bridle when standing on the near-side. Untie but do not at this stage remove the headcollar. Keep the horse tied-up to prevent him moving off*

Above: *Place the reins over the horse's head and neck and invite him to accept the bit by giving it with your left hand*

Above: *After placing the bit into the horse's mouth, take the headpiece over the ears. Check that the tongue of the horse is under the bit and that the bridle is in its correct position*

Above: *Finally tighten the bridle, and check the space between the horse's head and throatlash by placing three fingers between them. All buckles should be fitted and ends placed in the sleepers*

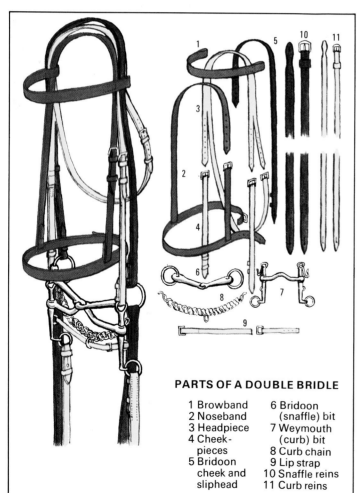

PARTS OF A DOUBLE BRIDLE

1 Browband	6 Bridoon (snaffle) bit
2 Noseband	7 Weymouth (curb) bit
3 Headpiece	8 Curb chain
4 Cheek-pieces	9 Lip strap
5 Bridoon cheek and sliphead	10 Snaffle reins
	11 Curb reins

Right: *The first horse illustrated is wearing a headcollar. The other three horses are wearing different types of bridle. The choice of bridle will depend on the experience of the rider, the horse's temperament, and the purpose for which the horse is being ridden*

Headcollar

Types of bit

Rubber snaffle

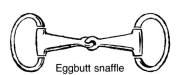
Eggbutt snaffle

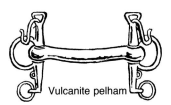
Kimblewick

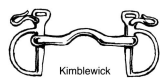
Vulcanite pelham

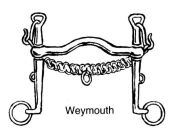
Weymouth

Bandages

Bandages are used in a number of different ways and for a variety of purposes. First, there is the tail bandage, made from elasticated or stretch material, and used to keep the tail looking neat and tidy. Never use a tail bandage at night, and always use a tail bandage with a tail guard when travelling.

Second, the stable bandage which gives both warmth and protection, and third, the exercise bandage which is used over gamgee or other tissue.

New varieties of bandages are made from cotton, wool, crepe, and other artificial fibres. Recently a type of stretch sock has become available. Other 'bandage-type' protection fastens, rather than being wound round the leg and then tied or sewn in place.

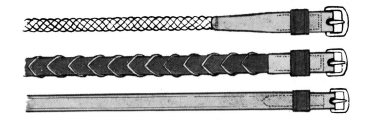

Above: *Three types of ordinary reins. From top to bottom: a Dartnell rein, a* *webbing rein, a plain leather rein (one of the most common)*

Right: *Before travelling, ensure the horse or pony is fully protected. Special tacking-up must be carried out before leaving for a show or for any other reason to travel. It is also essential to prepare a horse thoroughly before the return journey*

Snaffle

Double bridle

Pelham

Beginning to ride

Riding is not something which can be self-taught. Nobody can learn to ride by reading books about the subject, or by watching films or other people, or by getting on a horse and taking it from there! The best way to learn is to have lessons from qualified, trained instructors at a riding school or establishment. These pages give only an outline and should be studied *side by side* with your instruction.

From the first lesson, there is a great deal to absorb, and mistakes, when they occur, are best seen from the ground. One of the pleasures of learning is that you can make corrections while remaining mounted. By their very nature, early lessons may seem repetitive and boring, but the basic elements must be understood and applied before one can make progress. It is easy to become impatient and long to be able to ride out of the school. You must remember that every lesson brings that day nearer.

Part of the skill in riding is being able to 'feel' that things are right. This feeling comes through use of the correct **aids** – the body, seat, hands and legs.

The aids

The first of the two types of aids are known as the 'natural' aids. These are signals which are passed to the horse by the rider's use of the body, hands, legs and voice. The second group are known as the 'artificial' aids, those given by using a whip or spurs. Artificial aids are never used in early stages of riding. Even later on, they are not part of the younger rider's requirements to make a horse or pony responsive and obedient. The natural aids, however, must always be applied smoothly and quietly, with confidence and without any fuss.

Balance and impulsion

A horse or pony is said to be *balanced* when its weight, and that of the rider, is spread evenly. It can then move with ease and maximum efficiency. Too much *impulsion* (and sometimes too little) may result in loss

Left: *Two well-mounted younger riders shown during a break in a competition. Neither are using any of the 'artificial' aids.*
*The **voice** should always be used sparingly. Horses and ponies enjoy being talked to, but so often the voice of younger riders becomes almost a shout! Calmly and quietly encourage: quietly and firmly reprimand.*
*Once impulsion has been built up, the **hands** control forward movement. They are used with other 'natural' aids – body, legs and voice. Sympathetic hands are essential to good riding.*
*The **legs** of the rider, when correctly applied, help build up impulsion. They also guide and control the hindquarters*

What to wear

Whether in the stableyard, paddock or on the roads, it is sensible to have suitable clothing. This does not mean always being dressed as if for a show or competition, but certain items of clothing are essential.

The four main items are: a hard riding hat; a pair of trousers or jodhpurs; a jacket, sweater or anorak, and boots or shoes.

For most, the reasons for wearing a hard hat (and one that *fits*) are obvious. Accidents happen so suddenly, and more riders are killed or maimed through head injuries than for any other reason. It is strongly suggested that young riders wear a hard hat at all times, even when carrying out stable duties.

In Britain it is now a Rule that protective headgear, which includes a retaining harness secured to the shell of the hat at more than two points, must be worn with the *chinstrap fastened* at all showjumping events – even when in the practice area or collecting ring. The Pony Club movement have gone further: they make it compulsory to wear a hard hat or a jockey's skull cap, with a fastened chinstrap, at all Pony Club activities

Above: *Three well turned-out riders, under the watchful eye of their instructor, show that it is not only very new riders who undertake schooling and training lessons. Acquiring skill in riding means* *continual work, long after the basic instruction from a riding school or establishment*

Right: *Leathers are fitted to a saddle by using the 'bars'. These are metal fittings found on both sides*

of this balance, which is quickly felt by an experienced rider.

Impulsion is another word for the energy produced by a horse, once the rider has applied the correct aids. It does not mean speed. It is not an easy term to grasp, but it is best described as the energy produced by the horse when it is in active movement involving the entire body, especially its quarters or hocks. Correct sensing of a horse's impulsion is an important part of good jumping technique (p. 40).

Mounting

Horses and ponies, like many domesticated animals, do not always respond immediately to something new. Do not repeat the same lesson, but after a short time, change to something different, and then come back. Always avoid repetition.

One of the early lessons in training a horse or pony is to teach it to stand still at the halt. This is essential for safe and correct mounting or dismounting.

Before mounting, check the girth to see that it is secure. From the nearside, the horse is mounted with the rider's left shoulder against the horse's near shoulder. The rider takes the reins in the left hand, holds the nearside stirrup leather in the right hand and places the left foot into the stirrup iron. Make sure that the toe does not dig into the side of the horse when turning the body to face the saddle. Take hold of the cantle with the right hand. Keep hold of the reins with the left hand, and place it on the horse's withers. Swing the body up, moving your right hand to the front arch of the saddle and taking care not to kick the horse as the right leg goes over its quarters. Lower the body gently into the saddle and place the right foot into the stirrup. Sit well down and take up the reins in both hands. Check the girth again, as it may require adjustment and tightening (see illustration below).

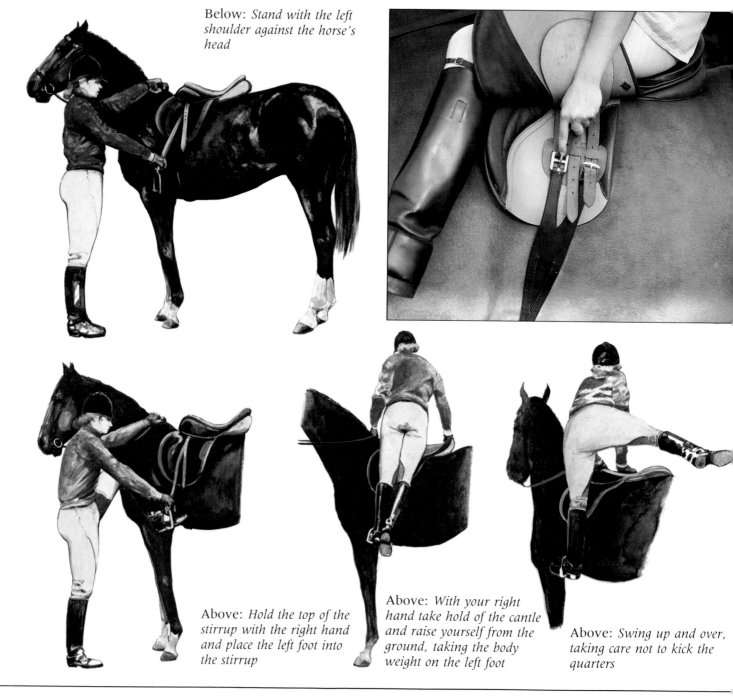

Below: *Stand with the left shoulder against the horse's head*

Above: *Hold the top of the stirrup with the right hand and place the left foot into the stirrup*

Above: *With your right hand take hold of the cantle and raise yourself from the ground, taking the body weight on the left foot*

Above: *Swing up and over, taking care not to kick the quarters*

Dismounting

To dismount, the rider does not simply reverse everything done on mounting. Once at the halt, remove both feet from the stirrups. Hold the reins firmly in the left hand and, turning the body, bring the right hand to the front arch of the saddle. Then, taking the body weight on the arms, swing the right leg over the horse's quarters and vault to the ground, landing on the toes. The rider will now be facing the nearside of the horse, still holding the reins in the left hand. Run-up the stirrups on both sides before slightly loosening the girth. Take the reins over the horse's head and lead away.

Right: *Remove both feet from the stirrups and take the reins in the left hand*

Right: *It is advisable to hold the pommel with the right hand when swinging the right leg over the quarters*

Right: *Vault to the ground, keeping hold on the reins, and land on the toes*

At the end of a ride

After riding out, and when a few hundred metres from your stable yard, it is a good idea to dismount, run-up the leathers, slightly loosen the girth, and walk your horse or pony quietly back. This will enable him to relax and cool down. However, you must not permit him to be lazy. You, the rider, must lead him with a good stride (even though you may feel tired) and you must see your horse is alert and enjoying having you off his back! Walk against oncoming traffic, keeping yourself between the traffic and the horse.

If you follow this procedure you will see why we emphasize the need to teach every horse to stand quite still when at the halt. It is one thing to dismount in the stable yard, when the horse knows he will be fed or allowed to run free and that the saddle and tack will be removed. It is quite another thing to dismount away from home and have a brisk, bright walk back to the yard.

Left, opposite: *Once mounted, adjust the girth by lifting the saddle flap and tighten each strap, using the index finger to guide the tongue of each buckle*

Below: *When carrying a whip it is correct for it to lie across the rider's thigh, pointing downwards as illustrated*

The paces

The four natural paces or gaits of a horse or pony are the walk, trot, canter and gallop. Advanced paces include the 'medium', 'collected', or 'extended'. In the United States a pace taken at a slow walk or slow trot is known as an amble. Changes from one pace to another are made by the rider's correct use of the aids (see page 32). Moving through the paces – the transition from one pace to another – demands a smooth movement of both horse and rider. Experienced dressage riders make the changes without the action of the hands or legs being too obvious.

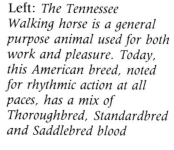

Left: *The Tennessee Walking horse is a general purpose animal used for both work and pleasure. Today, this American breed, noted for rhythmic action at all paces, has a mix of Thoroughbred, Standardbred and Saddlebred blood*

Above: *Hunter's Moon being ridden at a gallop by Mr Vin Toulson*

One important riding skill is to be able to make transitions and then *keep* at the selected pace, in other words to maintain pace. This is taught in riding schools. You should not leave the school area until you can manage this without too much difficulty. Three of the four natural paces are illustrated on page 37. There is a quite distinct number of 'beats' to each stride: the walk has four; the trot has two; the canter has three, and the gallop has four. Everyone who rides must be able to 'hear' the stride.

Collected walk: *This pace gives a shorter stride than the ordinary walk. Contact should be maintained, and the horse move with a raised head and unhurried pace*

Extended walk: *Here the horse strides out, yet must not be allowed to hurry or lose the regular rhythm of the pace. The rider keeps contact, allowing the horse to stretch and extend*

Free walk: *The rider 'gives' fully to allow the horse freedom of action. The reins must be slackened to allow easy movement, but the rider must maintain control*

WALK

After mounting, sit well down in the saddle, keeping the back straight but relaxed, and look ahead. The knees and thighs should remain close to the saddle, the lower parts of the legs lying along the line of the girth. Rest the balls of the feet in the stirrup irons, with the heels lower than the toes. Apply and keep a light contact with the horse's mouth. To move forward, squeeze the lower parts of the legs against the horse's sides, slightly behind the girth. Maintain contact with the hands and adjust body weight. Next, 'open' the hands, bringing the horse up to the bit, and move off. To bring the horse back to the halt, sit well into the saddle and straighten the spine. Close the lower parts of the legs and keep an even pressure with the hands. 'Close' the hands to bring the horse back to the bit. The pressure applied and the resistance felt through the bit brings the horse to the halt position. He should then stand quietly and square

TROT

To move from the walk to a trot, increase pressure with the lower part of the legs. Shorten the reins to bring the horse up to the bit. As he responds, squeeze the legs to hold the pace. Next ease the reins, but keep contact with the horse's mouth
Two ways of riding at a trot are the 'sitting' and 'rising' positions. The sitting trot is used when making the transition from the trot to another pace. In the rising trot keep a straight back and do not lean forward. Grip well with the thighs and knees. The legs remain against the horse's sides

CANTER

To move from the trot to the canter increase pressure with both legs behind the girth. Sit well down in the saddle and keep the horse well up to the bit. When cantering, keep close contact with the saddle. The horse should move into his stride with the foreleg leading. A horse is cantering 'disunited' or 'false' when, in moving to the left, the off-foreleg leads, or, if to the right, the near-foreleg leads. The incorrect use of the rider's body weight easily upsets the pace of the canter. Do not lean too far forward or full control will be lost and the horse will move on too quickly and unevenly. The canter is the most difficult pace to perform well, but both horse and rider will improve with experience

GALLOP
The gallop is a pace seldom used by the younger rider. In this pace the rider adopts a forward position, with his/her weight as near as possible to the centre of gravity. At all times the rider must be in control

Schooling

Horses at grass take exercise as and when they choose. Frequently, for no apparent reason, they will suddenly stop grazing, have a quick canter and probably a buck or two, and then, almost as suddenly, stop and resume grazing. This is the natural form of exercise for an animal to take, but it does mean horses and ponies at grass are sometimes hard to catch! To teach a horse to come to your call, or to respond to an invitation by offering something special to eat, is almost an impossible task. They remain totally independent, despite horse and rider getting on well once they come together!

Periods of schooling and exercising aim to teach obedience. They must also aim to make the horse or pony supple, and, at the same time, to build up its muscles to bring the animal into 'hard condition'. To achieve the best results from schooling, both horse and rider need to concentrate on the work in hand. Where possible, a horse or pony should be schooled in a quiet corner of the paddock, away from distractions such as other horses or a busy road.

Where there is no manège, it is a good idea to mark out a piece of level ground measuring 40 x 20 metres. This is the size of a normal dressage arena, and it makes an ideal area in which to school and practise. The rider can practise all sorts of changes of rein, make circles of differing diameters, make serpentines from one end to the other, and carry out the pattern of figures-of-eight (see diagram). This can all be done in a marked out space which keeps horse and rider concentrating on the work being done.

One of the problems which arise when schooling and exercising is how to avoid boring repetition. The amount of time to be given to one routine before moving on to something new needs great judgment, and becomes easier with experience. A short lesson is frequently more productive than a long, repetitive session.

Schooling need not be confined to the school or training area. On bridlepaths, or where space permits, make the horse or pony halt and then move forward through the paces. Teach it to stand still and square, and to await your signal to move off. In traffic there are many occasions when the horse and rider must be patient and wait for an opportunity to move on or make a turn. Be safe on the roads and you should always consider other road users. Remember: be seen, be vigilant, be safe.

Above, left: *Lungeing should not be attempted by the inexperienced. Watch a lungeing session by a qualified trainer, but do not attempt to copy this without experienced assistance. The object of lungeing is to teach quietness and obedience; to encourage the forward movement; to help develop muscles on both flanks of the horse or pony, and to create suppleness.*
When lungeing to the left, the trainer will take the lunge rein in the left hand and the lungeing whip in the right hand. These positions are reversed when lungeing to the right

Left: *One way to encourage balance and a smooth forward movement is to get a horse to walk over coloured poles on the ground. The distance between the poles will vary for one horse and another, but it may be best to start with the poles approximately 1.5 metres (5 feet) apart. The next stage, to teach horse and rider something about jumping, is to raise the poles by placing them on a brick or low-lying stand*

Below: *A manège, or area of level land measuring 40 x 20 metres, makes an ideal schooling area. Some of the many useful movements are illustrated here, including circles. The entire area may be used to great advantage*

Above: *Once competent in jumping low obstacles, a horse and rider may attempt well-built, solid-looking fences. This illustration shows a very good take-off position*

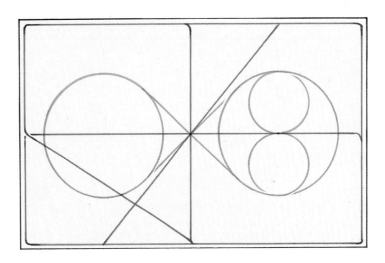

Jumping

Horses and ponies are, surprisingly, not 'natural' jumpers. They are, however, quite prepared to take advantage of any gaps in fencing or hedging! A young or 'green' horse has to be taught to jump even the most simple of obstacles. Less experienced riders are seldom mounted on a horse or pony which has not previously been trained to jump. This is of great help to the rider, although the horse must sometimes wonder what is in the mind of the person in the saddle!

Those learning to jump must be mounted on a *suitable* horse or pony, and will begin by walking, trotting and cantering over a line of poles, correctly spaced out and lying flat on the ground. This exercise encourages good balance and a safe seat, and teaches direction. Once poles lying flat can be negotiated, and the rider becomes more confident, they may be slightly raised on bricks or supports.

All riders know how easy it is for bad habits to take over, and how difficult they can be to correct. No jumping practice should therefore be attempted without someone standing by. Only a person on the ground can see what is going right – and wrong! And there is always the possibility of a fall.

The jumping position begins with shortened leathers, which keep the rider in the *lowest* part of the saddle. The hands adopt the normal riding position, maintaining contact and 'giving' with the horse's action and movement. Arms show a straight line from elbows to the horse's mouth.

Balance and impulsion must not falter as the obstacle is approached. The rider's head should remain still, with eyes looking ahead. The body must be straight and supple, with shoulders slightly forward of centre. The rider must always remain in balance and use his or her seat and body correctly. The illustration on page 41 shows the four phases of jumping: (from top to bottom) the approach, take-off, suspension and landing. Study the position of the rider's body, hands and legs in each phase, then look at the action of the horse.

The rider must make sure that the horse arrives at the correct spot in the approach. Any adjustments must be made prior to the final three strides. The horse should reach the point of take-off with slightly increased momentum – not too fast and not out of rhythm. In the final three strides, the rider should do nothing to affect the animal's concentration.

1 The approach

2 Taking-off

3 Suspension

4 Landing

Left, above: *Two types of obstacles or fences found in most novice or junior showjumping classes. These will also form part of most working hunter courses* Top: *A rustic gate.* Bottom: *A rustic fence with a brush on the approach side*

Left, opposite: *A young rider jumps clear at a Horse Trials at Chepstow, Wales, in 1989*

Above: *Stephen Smith, son of the famous rider Harvey Smith, shown coming down the Derby Bank, one of many unique obstacles at Hickstead in Sussex*

Right: *This sequence shows a horse in the four phases of jumping – the approach; take-off; suspension over the obstacle, and landing before moving off. The rider's position in the saddle is very important at each phase, and the hands must 'give' to allow the horse freedom to use his hocks, neck and body*

Showjumping

Showjumping is perhaps the most popular of all equestrian activities. It caters for all levels of ability and experience. The rules of the sport are not difficult to follow, and each national association produces annually its own Rules book. Owners and riders must study this book with great care, as changes and amendments are made each year.

Everyone involved in showjumping competitions, including those who watch, finds it a most exciting sport. The degree of precision and accuracy required means that many things can go wrong, so results are never certain; the most experienced combinations do not always win.

The methods by which competitions are judged vary. In some, competitors with an equal number of faults after one round will have to jump off 'against the clock', so the winner will have the fastest time and lowest number of faults. In 'speed' classes, the competitor with the fastest overall time will be the winner, since all disobediences are penalised by adding seconds to the time taken.

At all competitions the course designer prepares a plan of the course to be jumped. Every competitor should study this before they 'walk the course'.

Right: *An artist's impression of a course of 10 obstacles which might be set for a novice or junior showjumping class. After going through the start, Fence 1 is an inviting spread fence to encourage the horse or pony to go on. Fence 2 is an upright; Fence 3 an ascending spread; Fence 4 a gate; Fence 5 a combination, showing an upright leading into an ascending oxer; Fence 6 an upright of coloured poles; Fence 7 another combination, this time showing a parallel leading into an upright; Fence 8 another upright; Fence 9 a spread; Fence 10 a wall*

Below, right: *Competitors, officials and spectators stand for a national anthem at an international competition in the world-renowned showground at Aachen in Germany*

Bottom, left: *The famous rider David Broome and Lannegan, jumping at Hickstead in 1990*

One-stride distances

Care must be taken in determining the distance between elements in a one-stride combination. The measurements below are suitable for level ground and over good going. Jumping downhill requires distances to be *extended*: jumping uphill, the distances will require *shortening*. The minimum and maximum distances shown are for horses registered in Grade C. The pony distances are for ponies standing at 14.2hh.

Upright to upright
  Horses: 7.30m to 7.90m
  Ponies: 6.55m to 7.45m
Upright to parallel
  Horses: 7.15m to 7.60m
  Ponies: 6.55m to 7.15m
Upright to ascending oxer
  Horses: 7.00m to 7.60m
  Ponies: 6.55m to 7.15m
Parallel to upright
  Horses: 7.45m to 7.75m
  Ponies: 6.55m to 7.15m
Parallel to ascending oxer
  Horses: 6.85m to 7.30m
  Ponies: 6.55m to 7.15m
Ascending oxer to upright
  Horses: 7.34m to 7.90m
  Ponies: 6.55m to 7.15m

Below: *John Whitaker on Milton competing in the Nations Cup at Hickstead*

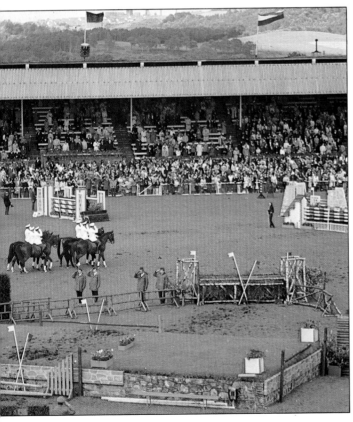

Dressage

The objects of dressage are to develop the physique and ability of the horse or pony, to improve its balance and suppleness, and to achieve harmony between horse and rider. Dressage has formed a basis for training horses and ponies for many centuries. Today it is accepted as an 'art' form which enjoys increasing support throughout the world. Like other equestrian sports, there are competitions for all levels of experience and ability – from basic tests to the demanding Grand Prix levels. Dressage is also the most valuable preparation for all forms of riding.

Judges of dressage have one of the most difficult of all judging tasks, as each movement has to be marked and comments added. The illustration shows how a dressage score sheet is prepared. At the end of the competition it is handed to the competitor for future reference.

Below: A score sheet showing how a judge might mark a dressage test at novice standard. The first column shows the number in the test. The second column gives the letters which make up the dressage arena (see below). The third column describes the particular test. Column four indicates the maximum marks for that part of the test, and column five the marks awarded. Finally, under 'observations' the judge will comment on each part of the test to help the rider in the future

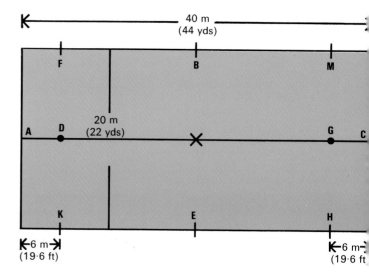

		Test	Max. Marks 1	Judge's Marks 1 to 10 2	Observations
1.	A X	Enter at working trot (sitting) Halt. Salute. Proceed at working trot (rising)	10	7	Straight entry. Quarters a little to left in halt. Smooth move off.
2.	C	Track right	10	6	More activity needed.
3.	A	Working trot (sitting) serpentine 3 loops, each loop to go to the side of the arena finishing at C	10	6	Coming above bit at times. Well shaped loops.
4.	M B BAE	Working trot right Circle right 20m diameter Working canter	10	8	Smooth strike off. Good circle.
5.	Between E&H K	Half circle right 15m diameter returning to the track between F&K Working trot (sitting)	10	4	Hollowing and becoming unbalanced before K. Trotted too soon.
6.	A C	Working trot (rising) serpentine 3 loops each loop to go to the side of the arena finishing at C Working trot (sitting)	10	6	Hollow in first loop, improving. Last loop good.
7.	H E EAB	Working canter left Circle left 20m diameter Working canter	10	7	Hind legs need to come underneath a little more.
8.	Between B&M F	Half circle left 15m diameter returning to the track between B&F Working trot (sitting)	10	7	Much better half circle. Canter well maintained.
9.	A KXM	Working trot (rising) Change rein and show a few lengthened strides	10	5	Hurried more than lengthened.
10.	C HXF	Medium walk Change rein at a free walk on a long rein	10	8	Good active free walk.
11.	F A G	Working trot (sitting) Down centre line Halt. Salute Leave arena at walk on a long rein at A	10	6	Straight down centre, but some resistance in mouth to halt.
12.		General impression, obedience and calmness	10	6	Not always round enough. Hind legs need bringing more underneath horse.
13.		Paces and impulsion	10	7	Smooth paces, needing a little more activity. Good walk.
14.		Position and seat of the rider and correct application of the aids	10	6	Fairly good position, but inclined to lean inwards on right rein.
		TOTAL	140	89	

Above: *A young competitor in the dressage arena at a 'local' one-day event*

Right: *A plan showing the markings of a dressage arena of normal dimensions*

Horse trials – eventing

The term 'horse trials' covers everything that comes under the heading of eventing. Eventing is recognized to be the most demanding equestrian activity. To take part in a one-, two- or three-day event, a horse and rider must possess not only skill in each of three phases, but also a close affinity, including confidence, obedience and trust. Obviously the fitness of both plays an important part, and success will only be achieved after thorough training. Another aspect of horse trials includes hunter trials, cross-country riding and combined training.

At a three-day event, the first day is devoted to dressage, the second day to Speed and Endurance, and the third day to showjumping.

The dressage test will normally take place in an arena measuring 40 x 20 metres (see page 39). A larger arena, 60 x 20 metres, is used for Advanced levels, for Grand Prix and at the Olympic Games.

Speed and Endurance covers four phases – A, roads and tracks; B, a steeplechase; C, further roads and tracks; D, cross-country. In phase A the horse and rider have to cover a distance varying between 3 and 8 kilometres at a set speed.

Above and left: *Three photographs showing phases which form part of a three-day event*

Top: *Dressage, showing a competitor at Grand Prix level*

Middle: *Showjumping, which demands precision and skill, follows the rigours of the Speed and Endurance phase the previous day*

Left: *Cross-country, where both horse and rider have to be courageous in tackling fixed obstacles and water hazards*

There will be an optimum time and a time limit, both shown on the course plan. In phase B, the steeplechase takes place over a course of natural-looking fences, extending to between 1½ and 3 kilometres. In phase C, the horse and rider face a further test over roads and tracks. In phase D, the cross-country course covers between 4 and 8 kilometres, including approximately 20 to 30 fixed and solid obstacles, plus water. Phase D is also taken at a set speed, with time playing an important role. Time penalties in all four phases are awarded to those who exceed the optimum time, but who are within the time limit. Penalties are awarded for all disobediences and falls, and three refusals means elimination from the competition.

At one-day events the three disciplines are condensed into one day. A two-day event includes a short steeplechase and some roads and tracks.

Results of horse trials are found by adding together the penalty points from each section. The winner is the competitor with the lowest final total.

For horse trials, both horse and rider must be very fit and well trained. Eventing demands a great deal of mental and physical effort, and a careful training programme is needed in preparation.

Right: *The origins of eventing go back to the days when the horse played an active role in military combat. Today, members of the armed forces compete successfully in horse trials throughout the world*

Far right: *Jumping one of the many different types of obstacles which face the eventer. The car, seen on the left, will belong to the judge of that obstacle*

Below: *Britain's Ginny Leng taking off at one of the obstacles at the Whitbreads Horse Trials, Badminton, in 1989*

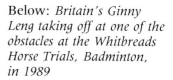

Below: *Water plays a big part in eventing. Here a competitor is seen after having jumped into a lake*

Right: *Anna Barrington clearing a solid-looking obstacle at a Junior Trials in Rotherfield Park, Hampshire*

Showing

Many owners enjoy the chance to exhibit in 'showing' classes. These classes are designed to cater for all types and breeds of horses and ponies, sometimes in separate age groups, and animals are presented to the judges either in hand (being led) or under saddle (being ridden). Some showing classes also take into account the rider's age and ability.

Working Hunter classes for either horses or ponies are particularly popular in some countries. In these, the competitor must show jumping prowess, combined with riding skill and technique. They must also give an individual display, showing the animal and themselves to best advantage.

American classes

American shows contain a wide range of specialized classes, involving both those who ride for fun and those who train horses to a very high level of skill. In Parade classes, riders are mounted on elaborately crafted saddles, with exotic bridles and other equipment. Western classes are also a distinctive feature of the American showing world.

Right: *A beautifully presented turn-out in one of the display classes popular at shows throughout the world. Note particularly the tack on the horse and the entire presentation. The whip (the person who drives) is in complete control*

Left, opposite: *A class specially for Shetland ponies – the smallest of the nine British native pony breeds*

Far left: *A judge assesses the pony's conformation before finally deciding on places in a showing class*

Left: *Prizewinners in a Hunter class show the high standard of turn-out needed for both horse and rider*

Right: *The first competition most young riders face is that for a Leading Rein class. This rider and pony, together with her helper on the leading rein, look confident and are well turned-out*

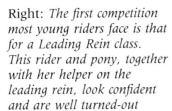

LEADERS

Main bar

lead bars or single bars

Crab

Head terret

Pole chain

WHEELERS

Carriage driving

In recent years there has been an increase in the numbers taking part in carriage driving competitions. Many others do not compete, but enjoy driving as a leisure activity.

Competitive carriage driving includes a variety of events, ranging from showing in *Concours d'elegance* classes to the testing three-phase trials. Trials consist of dressage, a marathon of approximately 25 kilometres in three or five sections (including various hazards to test the skill of the whip and the agility and obedience of the horses), and a twisting course of cones on which balls are balanced. This must be negotiated at speed.

Carriage driving has eight categories of competition for teams of four, pairs, tandems, singles. Classes are staged separately for either horses or ponies in each category.

Above: *Driving a single horse or pony, or a team of four, requires skilful handling. The illustration shows by the different colours how the reins are attached and used to a team of four. The reins are held in one hand by the whip, who through these controls pace, movement and direction*

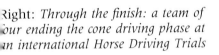

Near lead

Near wheel

Off wheel

Off lead

Right: Through the finish: a team of four ending the cone driving phase at an international Horse Driving Trials

Below left: The marathon: HRH Prince Philip in competition with a team of Fells owned by HM The Queen

Below, right: A pair being 'shown' to the judges during the dressage phase

Horseracing

Horses have been ridden in races against each other for centuries. Proper control and development of the sport in Britain began with the formation of the Jockey Club at Newmarket in 1751. Earlier in the 18th century, the English Thoroughbred was founded (p. 12). This breed is ideal for racing purposes, having great speed and stamina. Later, after exporting some descendants of the early Thoroughbreds, other countries developed breeds to be especially suitable for the racecourse.

Racing takes place in many countries, and falls into four broad categories – flat racing, steeplechasing, hurdling and trotting. Horses are trained to race over both left-handed and right-handed tracks. These, and the gallops, are made of sand, all-weather materials or grass. Excellent facilities have been created out of the deserts in Egypt, Dubai and Saudi Arabia. Steeplechasing and hurdling have always taken place in Britain and Ireland, and have spread to many other countries. Flat racing is universally popular, and trotting (harness racing) is also found in the United States and some European countries.

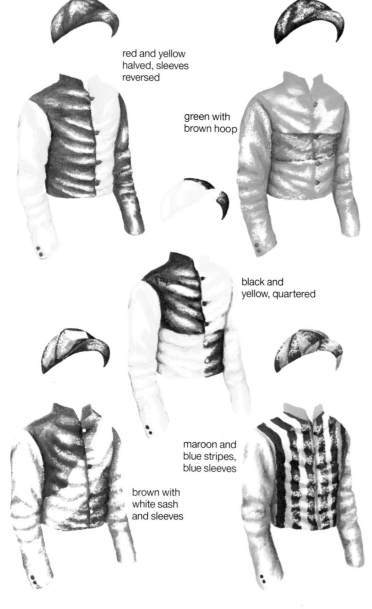

red and yellow halved, sleeves reversed

green with brown hoop

black and yellow, quartered

brown with white sash and sleeves

maroon and blue stripes, blue sleeves

Left: *The colours which identify each owner are worn both on the cap and jacket (shirt). These colours are still known as racing 'silks', though today they are usually made from man-made fibres. The bright colours and patterns are easy to distinguish during a race*

Below: *'They're off!' The shout that is heard as the starters leave the stalls. Only in flat races are starting stalls used: in steeplechasing and hurdling the starter indicates the start by raising the tape once the horses have approached in a straight line*

Opposite, below: *Rounding Tattenham Corner in the world's most famous flat race – the Derby, at Epsom in Surrey. The distances raced on the flat vary between 5 furlongs and 11 furlongs (a furlong being $\frac{1}{8}$ of a mile). Many races are handicaps, meaning that the horses on better form carry the greater weights, thus making it possible (but most unlikely) that all runners will finish level! A weight for age scale is also used as a basis of handicapping*

Above: *Hurdle racing began in the early part of the 19th century. It is held over varying distances. The height of each hurdle is 1.2 metres (3ft 6in) and there are not more than 4 hurdles in each mile raced*

Above right: *In harness racing (trotting), the horse maintains a specific gait while pulling a lightweight two-wheeled sulky in which the driver is seated. Harness racing may be the successor of chariot racing, known to have taken place more than 4000 years ago*

Right: *Steeplechasing is probably the most exciting of all forms of racing. The word was derived from the races whose courses lay from one church steeple to another. The fences look formidable, and, like hurdling, there are limits to the number of fences in each mile. In 'chasing, the number is set at 12 fences in the first 2 miles, and 6 in each additional mile. Some races cover distances exceeding 3 miles*

Some of the world's great races

In Britain, the *Triple Crown* is made up of the Derby, the Oaks and the Two Thousand Guineas. Other great races are the Oaks, St Leger and the King George VI and Queen Elizabeth Diamond Stakes. Three of the great races held in the United States are the Kentucky Derby, the Preakness Stakes and the Belmont Stakes.
Other great races include:
the Melbourne Cup of Australia, the Irish Sweeps Derby, the Prix de l'Arc de Triomphe, the Cheltenham Gold Cup, the Ascot Gold Cup, the Champion Hurdle and, of course the Grand National

Horses at work

The history of the working horse is closely linked to that of humans. For many thousands of years, the horse provided people with their only means of transport, and was especially important in hunting for food. Carvings from 1300BC in Egypt show the horse in use, and it has been an essential working animal throughout history.

Many associate the working horse with the 'heavy' horse, those cold-bloods which include the Shire, Clydesdale, Percheron, Jutland, Ardennais, Swedish Ardennes. Today, lightweight, or warm-blood horses and ponies, with Arab, Andulusian or Thoroughbred blood, are also working animals.

The use of horses for transport reached a peak in the 19th century. In Britain, horses were much the most important means of transport before the railways arrived in 1845. Horse-drawn coaches and carriages took people and goods from one place to another, and were very important in the early postal service.

Anyone who loves horses and ponies *must* study their history to see the development of these fine animals and their contribution over the centuries.

Above, left: *Horses are used to herd stock on the plains of North and South America. In Australia and New Zealand horses are used extensively in herding sheep and cattle. Here a stockman is collecting a calf. Both cowboy and stockman depend on the skill and intelligence of his horse, just as a shepherd does on his sheepdog*

Above, middle: *From the earliest times, horses and ponies have been used as beasts of burden. This German pack pony has a large box container strapped to either side of the saddle*

Left, bottom: *A police horse at work in traffic in central London*

Right, top: *Not many years ago the horse was the most important possession of a farmer. In 1910 there were more than 20 million horses working on the farms in the United States. 80 years later it was estimated that fewer than 6 million horses worked.*
Today horses still plough heavy soil in which tractors might become bogged down

Right, bottom: *Horses have always been used to haul many types of commercial and privately-owned vehicles. During the First World War a Corps of Women Drivers drove mail vans*

Below: *A horse-drawn 'gharry' works as a taxi in the busy streets of New Delhi, India*

Left: *One of the world-famous Lipizzaner stallions performing at the Spanish Riding School in Vienna. The School was founded during the 16th century, and is the oldest riding academy in the world*

Right: *One of the many great annual events held in London is the Cart Horse Parade. This takes place each spring in Regents Park, bringing together hundreds of horse-drawn vehicles. Some of these are still used daily on the streets of London*

Left, below: *Corporal Hurman of the Life Guards on Cicero, one of the most famous of all military horses*

Above right: *Jousting is now presented as a display at many horse shows. Originally it was a contest between two knights who opposed each other with lances*

Right: *For centuries, horses have performed in the circus. This picture shows the Crown Circus of Munich, one of the most famous in the world*

Left: *The rodeo dates back to the early part of the 19th century, when cowboys had learned the tricks needed to herd horses found in the wild. The first recorded rodeo, as a public spectacle, took place in Colorado in 1869*

Horses and sport

There are several ways in which horses and ponies are used for sporting activities, many of which have been discussed in previous pages. After careful and diligent training, the horse is a source of great enjoyment – even a leisurely hack across common land or exercising in a paddock can be a rewarding and pleasant pastime. Hunting, a sporting activity which can be traced over the centuries, involves following different types of hound, either mounted or on foot. It is widely practised in most horse-loving countries. Polo, said to be the oldest known sport in the world, is a game enjoying increasing popularity. Polo ponies are not a breed, but a special *type* of horse. They must be obedient, active and supple, and are trained to twist and turn in a very fast-moving sport. Other sporting uses of horses and ponies include side-saddle riding, long distance riding, trekking, trail riding, and a great variety of mounted games and gymkhana events.

Opposite, left: Many riders find a great enjoyment in hacking in lanes, on commons and riding along bridleways

Right: Pony trekking is a splendid way to enjoy a riding holiday. In most cases trekking starts from a riding centre, and returns home after a few hours away. More experienced, adventurous riders may decide to go long-distance trekking or trailing, on a ride extending over many miles and several days

Opposite, below left: Hunting is a traditional sport which arouses strong feelings in participants and opponents. Certain farmers and landowners allow hunts across their land, and the Hunt and its followers do everything possible to prevent damage to fences or crops. The quarry of hunts differs throughout the world, but in Britain and Ireland the most common form of hunting is with foxhounds. This illustration shows a Hunt going through a previously-opened gate

Right: No one knows quite how polo began, although there are records of games played in 600BC. It may have originated in China, but polo in the form we know today was probably first played in Iran. A polo ground measures 275 metres (300 yards) long by 145 metres (160 yards) wide. The goal posts are 25 metres (8 yards) apart. The game is made up of a number of chukkas, each lasting 7 minutes. At the end of a chukka a bell is rung. Between each chukka there is an interval of 3 minutes to allow for a change of ponies, and an interval of 5 minutes at half-time

Further Information

Aids The signals given by a rider to convey his/her instructions. The *natural* aids are the correct application of the rider's body, legs, hands and voice; the *artificial* aids are the whip, spurs and martingale

Brood mare A mare used for breeding purposes

Brushing When a horse strikes the fore or hind leg with the leg opposite, resulting in cutting and injury near the joint of the fetlock. Sometimes brushing is brought about by bad action or bad conformation. Damage can be avoided by the use of brushing boots

Brushing boots A form of protection against brushing (see above). Made from leather or stout cloth with a thick form of pad to go against the leg. Can be fixed with buckles and straps or other forms of fastening

Cast A horse or pony is cast when it lies down in its box or stable and is unable to rise. A common cause for this is when the box or stable is too small, or when the animal is lying close to a wall. The word 'cast' is also used when a horse has lost a shoe

Clench The end of a nail which holds the shoe to the hoof. Clenches are 'closed' by the farrier when hammering the end over and against the wall of the foot (see page 27)

Clips Clipping-out is essential for horses and ponies in work during autumn (fall) and winter months. If not clipped, horses will quickly lose condition should they sweat-up after work or exercise. The four types of clip are: the *blanket* clip; the *hunter* clip; the *trace* clip and the *full* clip

Colt An ungelded male horse up to four years of age

Curb chain A metal chain fitted to the curb of a double bridle or Pelham. This must lie flat in the groove of the horse's jaw and its action must be understood if discomfort or injury to the horse is to be avoided

Dam The female parent of a foal

Filly A female horse under the age of four years

Foal A colt up to the age of twelve months – a male foal is known as a colt-foal; a female is a filly-foal

Gelding A castrated male horse of any age

Halter A headcollar made from leather or webbing (or sometimes artificial fibre), used for leading or tying-up a horse or pony

Hands The word used when measuring height. Derived from the width of a man's hand, now universally agreed at 4 in (10 cm)

In hand Used when a horse or pony is being led. The opposite of in hand is *under saddle* (ridden)

Laminitis Inflammation or fever in the feet caused by too much fast work over hard ground or too much 'heating' feed. Sometimes brought about by too little exercise

Mare A female horse which has reached the age of four years

Nosebands One of the parts which make up a bridle, and include the cavesson, drop, Grackle, flash and Kineton

Numnah A sheepskin, felt, nylon or rubber pad which fits under a saddle

Over-reach boots Circular rubber boots fitted to prevent injury when a horse over-reaches (see below)

Over-reaching When the edge or rim of the hind show strikes the coronet of the foot in front

Plaiting (sometimes known as *braiding*) is the process of making plaits to smarten overall appearance of the horse or pony before entering into competition. The number of plaits will vary, but tradition has it that there should always be an uneven number with one at the forelock. Tails are also plaited and protected when travelling by the use of a tail guard

Pulse The pulse rate of a horse is normally 36–40 beats to the minute

Risen clench When a clench rises and comes through from the wall of the foot. This is liable to cause injury and must be dealt with immediately it is noticed. One of the reasons for a *daily* check on horse's feet is to look for risen clenches

Shelter An open-sided hut or shed should be placed in every field where horses and ponies graze. This provides a place where the animals can go in summer to get out of the heat and away from flies, and in winter time to shelter from rain or severe weather. It must be sited so that the back wall is taking prevailing winds

Sire A stallion. A foal's male parent

Splint A bony growth between the splint bone and the cannon bone

Stallion A horse, not under four years of age, used for breeding

Yearling A colt or filly up to one year of age

Index